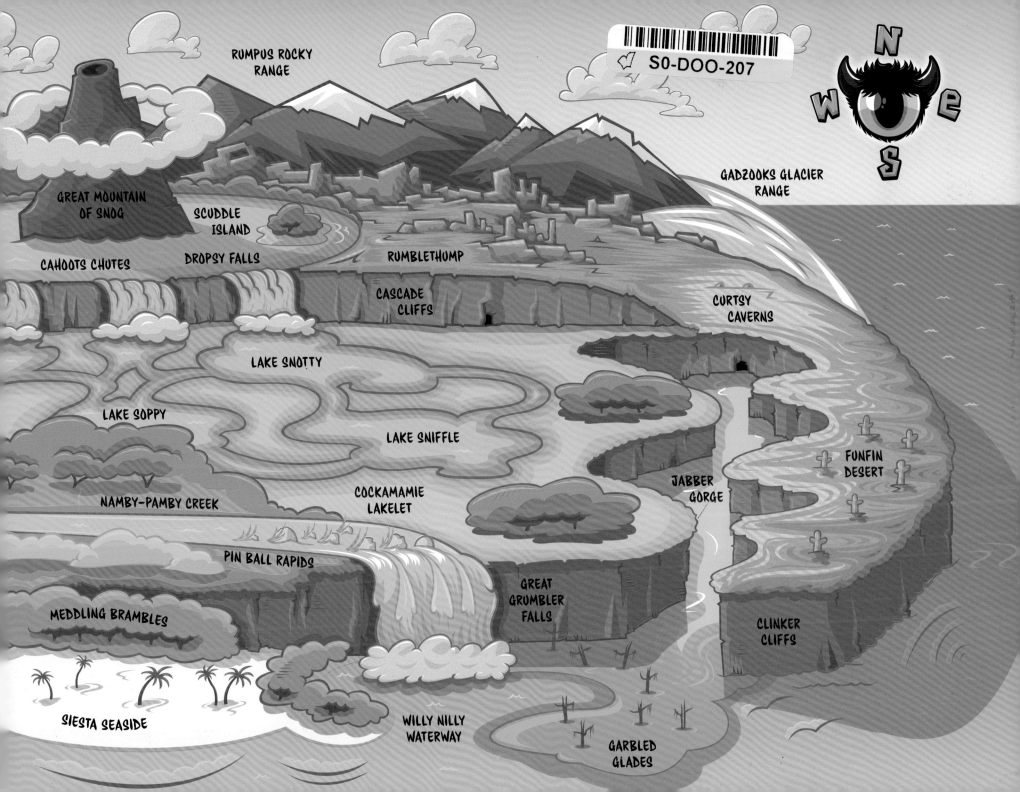

Published by

Explorers Playground Inc.
Los Angeles, CA

Text and Illustration Copyright 2014 by Explorers Playground Inc.

The fonts Tiki Magic, Custom, Sign, and Poster are © and ™ by House Industries

We would like to sincerely express our gratitude to
our Kickstarter contributors for believing in us
and helping to make this book a reality.
We owe its creation to your generosity.
We are truly humbled by all of your support.

Monster Hugs,
Meeks, Zapp, Hux, Mosby and The Nimblets!!!

Distributed by
Explorers Playground Inc
PO Box 1006 Agoura Hills, CA 91376

ISBN: 978-0-9886034-1-7
First Edition 2014
Printed in China

Website – www.horndribbles.com
Email inquires and questions: info@horndribbles.com

The Horndribbles: MEEKS™ AND THE GREAT INVENTION!

by Herbert Joel

MEET THE HORNDRIBBLES

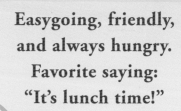

Strong and compassionate,
not to mention a great cuddler.
Favorite saying: "It's storytime!"

Easygoing, friendly,
and always hungry.
Favorite saying:
"It's lunch time!"

The best athlete on
Horndribble Island. Just ask him.
Favorite saying: "It's playtime!"

Hi, I'm Annabelle. I'd like to share a story with you.

It's about Meeks, Mosby, Zapp, and Hux.

They live deep in the Waka Forest on Horndribble Island.

Are you ready to hear one of my favorite adventures?

Here we go!

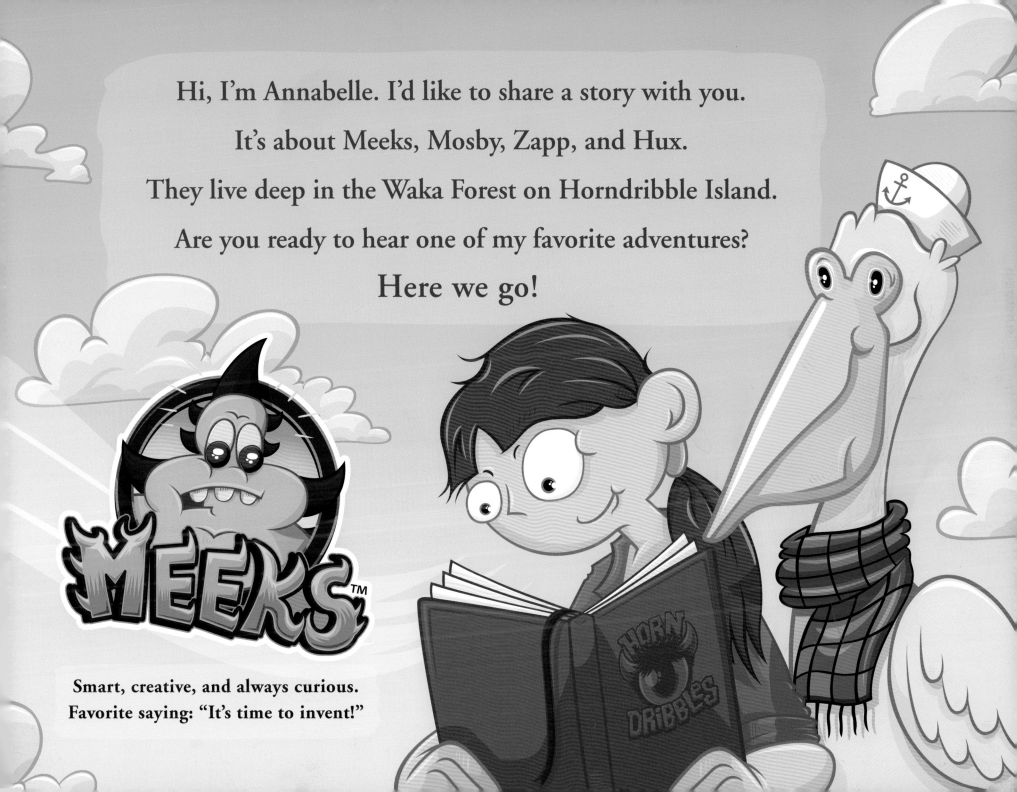

MEEKS™

Smart, creative, and always curious.
Favorite saying: "It's time to invent!"

One fine day Meeks, Mosby, Zapp, and Hux went to Fuddy-Duddy Fields to challenge their rivals to a game of Blue-Bang Ball.

They waited a long time, but
the other team never showed up.

"We can't play the game with just the four of us!" grumbled Hux.

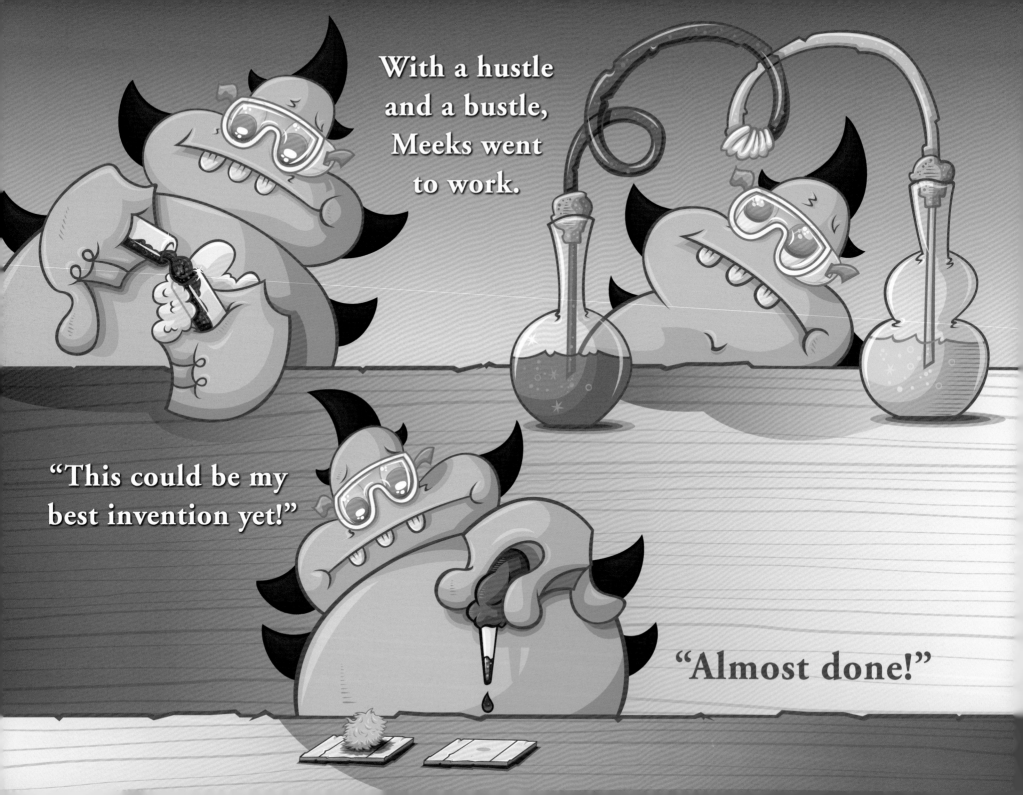

With a hustle
and a bustle,
Meeks went
to work.

"This could be my
best invention yet!"

"Almost done!"

Just then, Meeks' friends walked in.

"What are you doing in here?"
asked Hux.

Meeks panicked.
"We have to find them! It can
be dangerous out there!"
he said desperately.

The Horndribbles searched everywhere,
but there was no sign of
the Nimblets until...

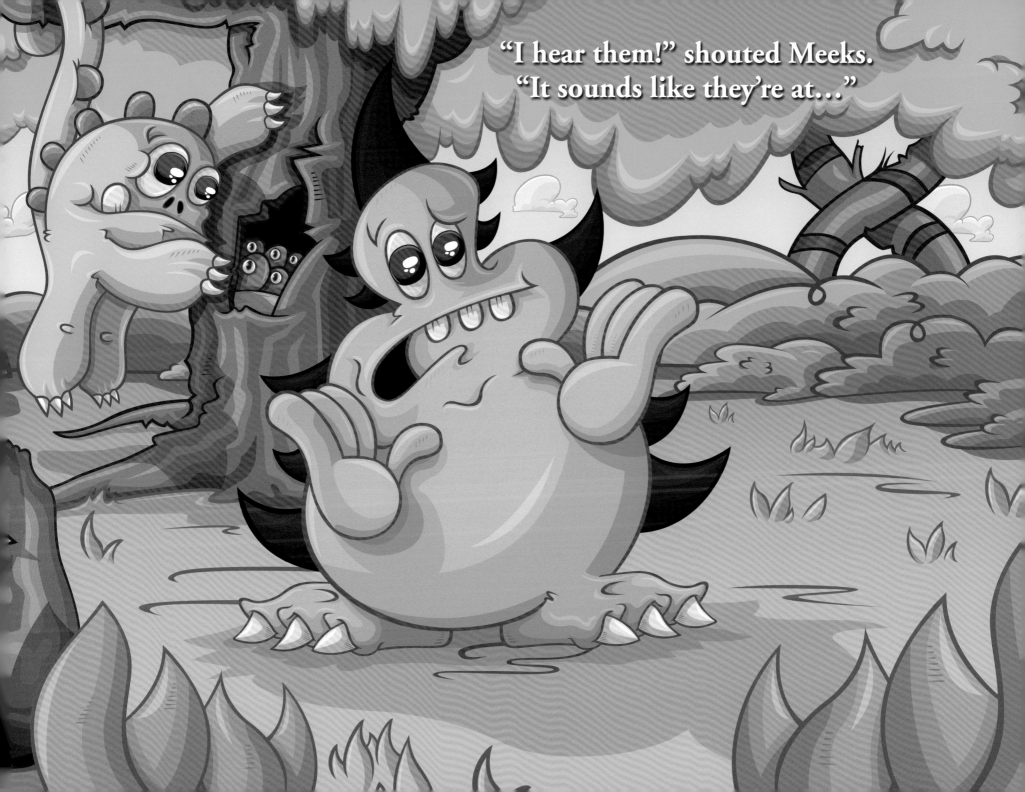

"I know how to get them,"
said Meeks. "I'll be right back."

Meeks quickly returned.
"Make way for the Net-O-Rang!"
he shouted.

"Wow, Meeks! Your Net-O-Rang sure did the trick," said Zapp. "I like our new friends," chimed Mosby.

"And now we have enough players for Blue-Bang Ball," said Hux.

"Hooray!" they all cheered.

I can't wait to see what adventures they have for us next.
Until then...